W9-CBP-679

The Cam Jansen Series

Cam Jansen and the Mystery of the Stolen Diamonds
Cam Jansen and the Mystery of the U.F.O.
Cam Jansen and the Mystery of the Dinosaur Bones
Cam Jansen and the Mystery of the Television Dog
Cam Jansen and the Mystery of the Gold Coins
Cam Jansen and the Mystery of the Babe Ruth Baseball
Cam Jansen and the Mystery of the Circus Clown
Cam Jansen and the Mystery of the Monster Movie
Cam Jansen and the Mystery of the Carnival Prize
Cam Jansen and the Mystery at the Monkey House
Cam Jansen and the Mystery of the Stolen Corn Popper
Cam Jansen and the Mystery of Flight 54
Cam Jansen and the Mystery at the Haunted House
Cam Jansen and the Chocolate Fudge Mystery
Cam Jansen and the Triceratops Pops Mystery
Cam Jansen and the Ghostly Mystery
Cam Jansen and the Scary Snake Mystery
Cam Jansen and the Catnapping Mystery
Cam Jansen and the Barking Treasure Mystery
Cam Jansen and the Birthday Mystery
Cam Jansen and the School Play Mystery
Cam Jansen and the First Day of School Mystery

Young Cam Jansen and the Dinosaur Game
Young Cam Jansen and the Missing Cookie
Young Cam Jansen and the Lost Tooth
Young Cam Jansen and the Ice Skate Mystery
Young Cam Jansen and the Baseball Mystery
Young Cam Jansen and the Pizza Shop Mystery
Young Cam Jansen and the Library Mystery
Young Cam Jansen and the Double Beach Mystery
Young Cam Jansen and the Zoo Note Mystery

Cam Jansen and the Tennis Trophy Mystery

David A. Adler
Illustrated by Susanna Natti

Viking

VIKING
Published by Penguin Group
Penguin Young Readers Group,
345 Hudson Street, New York, New York 10014, U.S.A.
Penguin Books Ltd, 80 Strand, London WC2R ORL, England
Penguin Books Australia Ltd, 250 Camberwell Road, Camberwell,
Victoria 3124, Australia
Penguin Books Canada Ltd, 10 Alcorn Avenue, Toronto, Ontario, Canada M4V 3B2
Penguin Books (N.Z.) Ltd, 182-190 Wairau Road, Auckland 10, New Zealand

First published in 2003 by Viking,
a division of Penguin Young Readers Group.

3 5 7 9 10 8 6 4

LIBRARY OF CONGRESS CATALOGING-IN-PUBLICATION DATA
Adler, David A.
Cam Jansen and the tennis trophy mystery / David A. Adler ;
illustrated by Susanna Natti.
p. cm. — (A Cam Jansen adventure ; 23)
Summary: Cam Jansen, with Eric at her side, helps solve the mystery of
what happened to Mr. Day's tennis trophy.
ISBN 0-670-03643-9 (hardcover)
[1. Lost and found possessions—Fiction. 2. Tennis—Fiction. 3.
Teachers—Fiction. 4. Mystery and detective stories.] I. Natti,
Susanna, ill. II. Title.
PZ7.A2615Caqm 2003
[Fic]—dc21
2003005315

Printed in USA
Set in New Baskerville

To Devorah, Shmuel, and Elana
—D. A.

To Selma and Whit Patrick
—S. N.

GO TEAM

CHAPTER ONE

"Something smells really bad," Cam Jansen whispered.

"We're in gym," Cam's friend Eric Shelton told her. "It always smells bad here."

"It's not a gym smell," Cam said. "It's worse."

Cam and Eric were standing on their spots. Mr. Day, their gym teacher, was checking attendance.

"I saw Danny get off the bus this morning," Mr. Day said. "I wonder why he didn't come to gym."

"Here I am."

"Danny is not on his spot," Mr. Day said quietly, and made a mark in his book. "And if he's not on his spot, he's absent."

"I am on my spot," Danny said, and quickly moved.

"Oh, there you are," Mr. Day said.

Mr. Day closed his marking book. He unlocked his office door and put the book away. Then he came out with his hands over his head. "Hands up," he called out. "Reach for the sky."

Everyone in the class reached up and stretched.

"Hands together. Feet apart."

The children put their hands together and moved their feet apart.

"Now," Mr. Day told the class. "Do jumping jacks."

Cam and her classmates jumped again and again. They jumped first with their feet apart and their hands together above their heads. Then they jumped and moved their feet together and their hands to their sides.

Most of the children jumped on their spots. Danny didn't. Each time he jumped, he bumped into someone else.

"Hey, watch out!" Eric said.

"Ow!" Cam told Danny. "You landed on my foot."

"Jump quietly!" Mr. Day called out.

Cam and Eric tried to be quiet. But Danny kept bumping into them.

"Ow again!" Cam said, and fell to the floor. "That's the second time you landed on my foot."

Eric and Danny stopped jumping. "Are you okay?" they asked Cam.

"Why are you talking? Why aren't you jumping? Don't you know the rules in this gym?" Mr. Day asked the three children.

"I do," Cam, Eric, and Danny said.

"Danny, read rule seven aloud."

Both boys turned to face the large sign on the wall of the gym. Cam didn't turn to face the sign.

"When you enter this room," Danny read from the sign, "go directly to your assigned spot. Remain there for attendance and exercises."

"Eric, read rule eleven aloud."

"Exercise time is *not* play time."

"Turn around," Mr. Day told Cam. "Face the sign and read rule fourteen aloud."

"I don't need to see the sign," Cam said. "I can read it from the picture of the sign I have in my head."

People say Cam has a photographic memory. They mean Cam's mind takes pictures of whatever she sees. Whenever she wants to remember something, she just looks at the picture stored in her head.

Cam closed her eyes and said, *"Click!"*

Whenever Cam wants to remember something, she says, *"Click!"*

"My mind is like a camera," Cam says, "and cameras go *click*!"

"Rule fourteen," Cam said with her eyes still closed. "This gym is a place for quiet exercise and play. A quiet gym is a safe gym."

Cam's real name is Jennifer Jansen. But when people found out about her amazing memory, they called her "The Camera." Soon "The Camera" was shortened to "Cam."

"While the class plays volleyball," Mr. Day told Cam, Eric, and Danny, "you will stand against the wall in the corner opposite the sign. You will study the sign. Maybe then you'll remember the rules."

"Cam remembers the rules," Eric whispered as they walked slowly to the side of the gym. "She remembers everything."

"What's that?" Mr. Day asked. "What did you say?"

"Nothing," Eric answered.

Mr. Day divided the class into two teams. He set one team on each side of the net. He stood on the side of the court.

"It's worse here," Cam whispered.

"What is?" Eric and Danny asked.

"The smell," Cam answered. "It's worse here. I think it's coming from Mr. Day's office."

CHAPTER TWO

"Pass the ball forward," Mr. Day told children in the back row. "Play as a team."

"I think it's coming from Mr. Day's office," Cam whispered to Eric.

"Sh," Eric said. "Don't talk. We're in enough trouble."

A boy in the back row hit the ball straight up. Everyone watched the ball go up. It almost touched the ceiling. Then they all watched the ball come down. No one tried to hit it.

"Don't just watch!" Mr. Day shouted to the children. "This isn't a television show. This is a game."

Cam quietly stepped closer to Mr. Day's office.

It was Janet Teller's turn to serve. She held the volleyball in her left hand. She made a fist with her right hand and hit the ball. It flew to the side, right at Mr. Day.

"Oh no," Janet screamed.

Mr. Day put his hands in front of his face and caught the ball.

Cam stepped even closer to the office.

Eric took a step, too. Then he whispered to Cam, "What are you doing?"

Mr. Day stood next to Janet.

"Hey," Danny called to Cam and Eric. "Where are you going?"

"Whisper!" Eric told Danny.

Danny moved next to Eric and whispered, "Where are you going?"

"Cam wants to know why there's a strange smell coming from Mr. Day's office."

"Maybe he's cooking garlic," Danny said. "Or maybe he's burning old sneakers. That would *really* stink."

Mr. Day held the ball in his left hand. "When you serve, hit the ball like this," Mr. Day told Janet. Then he took an even swing and hit it high over the net.

Cam took one more step and was by the office. She turned and looked through the small window in the door.

It was a small office. When Cam looked through the window, all she could see was

Mr. Day's desk and the old cabinet behind the desk.

The desk was piled high with papers.

The cabinet was against the back wall of the office. The cabinet had two locked glass doors. Cam looked through the glass doors to the back wall. It was painted yellow.

"That's it," Cam said. "That's the smell. The office was just painted. It was blue before and now it's yellow."

"Yellow!" Danny said.

Eric and Danny looked though the window.

"It's a big square banana. That's what it is," Danny said. "Mr. Day's office is a big square yellow banana."

"The cabinet looks a little empty," Cam said, and looked through the window again. "I think something is missing."

Cam closed her eyes and said, *"Click!"*

"That's it," Cam said with her eyes still closed. "That's what's missing."

Cam opened her eyes and looked at the top shelf of the cabinet. On the shelf were two silver trophies.

"He had three trophies on the top shelf," Cam said. "Now he just has two. His tennis trophy is missing."

CHAPTER THREE

"That's the trophy he won at last year's teachers' tournament," Eric said. "He's so proud of that one."

"Bam! Whoosh!" Danny said, and pretended to be swinging a tennis racket. "He beat Ms. Green."

"Maybe the trophy is in his desk," Eric said. "Maybe he took it home."

Mr. Day turned. He saw Cam, Eric, and Danny standing by the door to his office.

"I told you to study the rules," he said. "You can't see the sign from there."

"How did that happen?" Danny asked as

he looked to his right and looked to his left. "How did we get here?"

Cam, Eric, and Danny went back to the corner. They looked straight ahead at the sign.

"I've got to get in there," Cam whispered. "I've got to get in that office and look for that trophy."

"It's time to stop playing. Line up, please," Mr. Day told the class. He stepped forward and caught the volleyball. "You, too," he called to Cam, Eric, and Danny.

The children hurried to the entrance to the gym. They got in line and waited for their teacher, Ms. Benson.

"What happened to your tennis trophy?" Cam asked as she walked past Mr. Day.

"I won that last year," Mr. Day said. He was very proud of that trophy. "I won it in the teachers' tournament. The last match was real close. It was between me and Ms. Green." Mr. Day smiled. "She just couldn't hit my serve."

"Yes, she could," Danny said. "She thought the serve was out."

Mr. Day turned. He glared at Danny.

"Dr. Prell was the umpire, and she said it was good."

"After the tournament," Janet said, "that's all Ms. Green talked about, that the ball was out."

Now Mr. Day glared at Janet.

Ms. Benson walked into the gym. She spoke to Mr. Day for a moment. Then she led the children back to their classroom.

Cam didn't follow Ms. Benson.

"I know how you won the trophy," Cam told Mr. Day. "I want to know where it is. Did you put it on your desk? Did you take it home?"

"No," Mr. Day answered. "It's in my office, in the cabinet."

"No it's not."

Mr. Day walked to his office. Cam followed him. Mr. Day unlocked the door.

"Oh my," Mr. Day said. "It's gone."

There was a padlock on the glass doors to the cabinet. Mr. Day checked it. It was locked.

"I keep the office door and the cabinet doors locked. How could anyone have taken it?" Mr. Day asked.

"Maybe you took it home," Cam said.

Mr. Day pushed some papers aside and sat on the edge of his desk. He shook his head and said, "No."

Some papers on Mr. Day's desk fell to the floor. Cam put them back on his desk.

Mr. Day sat quietly. Cam looked at the cabinet. Then she turned and looked at the office door.

"Who else has the keys to your office?" Cam asked.

"Dr. Prell and Jake."

Dr. Prell was the school principal. Jake was the custodian.

"Do you ever leave the cabinet open?"

"No," Mr. Day said, and shook his head. "My trophies are valuable. They're real silver. That's why I keep the cabinet locked. And I keep tests and my marking book in there. I don't want someone to get them."

Cam looked at the cabinet. The two doors were closed. There was a padlock between the doors, and it was locked.

Someone broke into a locked cabinet, Cam thought, *and stole a silver trophy. And whoever did it put the lock back on. Why would the thief put the lock back on?*

Cam told Mr. Day, "I'm good at solving mysteries. Right now I'm having trouble with this one. But don't worry. I'll solve it."

"No you won't," Mr. Day told Cam. "You'll go back to class."

"But what about your silver trophy?"

"Don't you worry," Mr. Day said. "I'll find it."

No you won't, Cam thought as she walked to class. *I will.*

CHAPTER FOUR

"Where have you been?" Ms. Benson asked when Cam walked into class.

"I was in gym," Cam said. "I was talking with Mr. Day."

Ms. Benson told Cam, "We're learning about oceans." Then she asked, "Janet, please tell Cam what we learned."

"Almost three-fourths of the earth is covered with oceans," Janet read from her notebook. "There are five oceans, the Atlantic, Pacific, Indian, Arctic, and Antarctic, and they're all connected."

Cam sat in her seat. She opened her notebook.

Ms. Benson asked, “What causes waves?”

“Parents do,” Danny called out. “If your parents have wavy hair, so will you.”

“Adam,” Ms. Benson said. “Please tell Danny and Cam what causes waves.”

“It’s the wind,” Adam said. “And the moon causes tides.”

A folded piece of paper landed on Cam's open notebook.

"It's from me," Eric whispered.

"Cam," Ms. Benson asked, "do you know how the moon causes tides?"

Do I? Cam wondered. *I think I do. I think I read about it last night.*

Cam closed her eyes and said, *"Click!"* She looked at the pictures she had in her head of the page she had read in her textbook on oceans and tides.

"The moon's gravity pulls on the water," Cam said. "As the earth turns, it pulls on water over different parts of the earth. That's why we have high tides and low tides."

"Thank you," Ms. Benson said. "Now please open your eyes and pay attention."

Cam opened her eyes. She wanted to open Eric's note, too, but she waited.

Ms. Benson talked about currents. She also talked about plants and animals that live in the sea. Then she turned to write on the board.

Cam opened Eric's note.

"No," Cam whispered.

Ms. Benson wrote, ***Benthos are plants and animals that live at the bottom of the ocean.***

While Cam copied that, another note landed on her notebook. Cam opened it.

"No," Cam whispered.

Plankton, Ms. Benson wrote on the board, ***are plants and animals that float and drift in the ocean. Jellyfish are one kind of plankton.***

Eric was writing another note.

"Stop writing notes," Cam whispered.

Eric said, "Then tell me what happened."

Cam nodded. She wrote a long note about the missing trophy and the locked cabinet.

I don't know how someone got into the cabinet,

she wrote at the end of the note,

and why whoever stole the trophy locked the cabinet again.

Ms. Benson turned. ***Nekton,*** she wrote on the board, ***are animals that swim in the water.***

While Ms. Benson wrote about nekton, Cam folded her note and tossed it to Eric.

"Please," Ms. Benson said to the class, "copy what I have written on the board. Then we'll have silent reading."

Cam and Eric copied Ms. Benson's notes. Then they opened their books. Cam was reading a mystery.

In the book she was reading, diamonds were stolen from a jewelry store. The store was in a busy shopping mall. It was the middle of the day, and still the thief got away.

But Cam had trouble reading. She kept thinking about the missing trophy.

"That's it!" Eric said. "I've solved the mystery."

CHAPTER FIVE

"Please, read quietly," Ms. Benson told him. She was reading, too.

"I'm sorry," Eric said.

He took out his notebook and wrote a note. He waited for Ms. Benson to look in her book again. Then he tossed the note to Cam.

I solved the mystery

was written on the outside of the note

Cam looked at Eric. *Did he read my book? How does he know who stole the diamonds?* Cam wondered. *How does he know how the thief got away in the busy shopping mall?*

"Read my note," Eric whispered.

"Cam and Eric," Ms. Benson called out. "Please come here."

"What should you be doing now?" Ms. Benson asked.

"Reading," Eric said.

"But you've been writing and passing notes," Ms. Benson said. "And not just one note. It started just as soon as Cam sat down."

"You saw all that?" Cam asked.

"Yes," Ms. Benson said. "I saw all that. I know you remember everything. Well, in this class I *see* everything. Now tell me. What's going on?"

Cam told Ms. Benson about the trophy.

"That's terrible," Ms. Benson said. "Mr. Day is very proud of his trophies."

"It's a double mystery," Eric said. "Who took the trophy, and after he took it, why did he lock the case?"

"No," Cam said. "It's a triple mystery. "If he doesn't have a key to the lock, *how* did he lock the case again?"

Ms. Benson smiled. "Maybe I know why he locked the case again."

"You do?" Cam and Eric both said.

Ms. Benson explained. "The thief could have simply broken the glass door and taken the trophy. But for some reason he didn't want anyone to notice there was a theft. At least not right away. Somehow he unlocked the case and then, after he took the trophy, he locked it again."

"I know that," Eric said. "And I know how he did it."

Ms. Benson added, "It's easy to break some locks, but it's impossible to use them again."

"I know that! I know that!" Eric said. He told Cam to show Ms. Benson the note. "I solved that part of the mystery."

Cam gave the note to Ms. Benson.

"After the thief broke the lock," Ms. Benson read from the note, "he took out the trophy and then put another lock on the cabinet."

"He couldn't put the same lock on," Eric explained, "because it was broken."

"That makes sense," Cam said.

"Mr. Day won't be able to open the cabinet," Eric said. "It's a different lock, so his key won't work."

“Can we go to the gym to tell Mr. Day?” Eric asked.

“Yes, you may,” Ms. Benson said.

When they were in the hall, Cam said to Eric, “Even if you’re right, we still don’t know who stole the trophy.”

“But we know *how* he stole it and that’s a start,” Eric said. “And I’m the one who got us started.”

CHAPTER SIX

A fourth grade class was in the gym. They were playing volleyball.

"Did you forget something?" Mr. Day asked Cam and Eric.

"No," Eric said, and told Mr. Day about the locks.

"We'll try your key," Cam said. "If Eric is right, it won't open the lock."

"No," Mr. Day said. "*I'll* try the key. This class is leaving soon. Then we'll go into my office and *I'll* try the key."

Cam and Eric sat by the wall near Mr. Day's office.

"It's cold in here," Eric said, "and windy."

Cam pointed and said, "Mr. Day has the door open."

Mr. Day turned and looked at Cam and Eric.

Cam whispered, "He wants us to be quiet."

"And I feel like we're being punished again," Eric whispered.

Cam and Eric watched the game.

"This is boring," Eric whispered. "Why doesn't he just give us his keys and let us try the lock?"

"He keeps his marking book and tests in the cabinet. He doesn't want us to see them," Cam said. "That's why he won't give us the key."

"Pass the ball forward," Mr. Day told the class. "Play as a team."

A boy held the ball in his left hand. He swung his right hand back and hit the ball. It flew into the back of the head of the girl in front of him.

"Hey!" she yelled. "That hurt!"

"Hit the ball up," Mr. Day told the boy. "Hit it over the net."

This time the boy hit the ball too high over the net. It went straight up and hit the ceiling.

"He's worse than I am," Eric whispered.

"Okay," Mr. Day called out. "That's it. It's time to line up."

After the class left the gym, Mr. Day came over to Cam and Eric. "Let's try my key," he said.

"The key won't fit," Eric said. "Then all we have to do is find out whose lock is on the cabinet. Once we find him, we'll have the thief."

Mr. Day unlocked the door to his office. When he opened it a gust of wind blew papers off Mr. Day's desk.

Cam and Eric took some of the papers from the floor and put them on Mr. Day's desk.

"Leave them," Mr. Day said. Then he looked at the cabinet and said, "It looks like my lock."

"Sure it does," Eric said. "That was the whole idea. The thief wanted it to look the same."

Mr. Day put the key in the padlock. He turned the key. It opened the lock.

"I thought I solved the mystery," Eric said.

"Well, you didn't," Mr. Day said. "I still don't have my trophy."

Mr. Day took a pile of papers from a lower shelf of the cabinet.

"What are those?" Eric asked.

"Tests," Mr. Day told him. "These are tests on the rules of volleyball. I'm giving them next week."

"The thief left the tests," Eric said. "That proves he wasn't a student."

"No it doesn't," Cam said. "He could

have taken one copy of the test and left the rest."

Mr. Day looked at the pile of tests.

"Oh, my! That's true," Mr. Day said. "I'll have to make new tests."

Cam, Eric, and Mr. Day stared at the cabinet.

"It's not just the trophy," Mr. Day said. "It seems someone has a key to my office and to my cabinet. Now nothing I have in here is safe."

"I think you should get a new lock," Cam said.

Mr. Day unlocked the bottom drawer of his desk. "I think you're right," he said, "but until then, I'm putting everything in here."

Mr. Day took a lunch bag and a thermos from the drawer. He put the tests in. Cam and Eric took the two trophies still in the cabinet. They gave them to Mr. Day. He put them in the drawer, too.

There were still some books and papers in the cabinet.

"You can leave those," Mr. Day said. "They're not valuable. And anyway, there's no more room in here."

Mr. Day locked the drawer.

"What do we do now?" Eric asked.

"The painters took my posters off the walls," Mr. Day said. "You can help me put them back up."

There was a pile of posters on the floor. The top one was a picture of two Olympic champions and the message, EAT RIGHT. PLAY FAIR. BE A CHAMPION.

Cam and Eric helped Mr. Day tape that poster and several others to the wall.

“Thank you,” Mr. Day said. “My office looks better now.”

Cam looked at the walls. The posters looked great. Very little of the newly painted yellow walls was showing. Cam looked at the cabinet. She looked through the glass doors.

“Look at that,” Cam said. “I should have thought of it before. Look through the glass doors and you’ll know how the thief took the trophy. You’ll know why after he took it, the cabinet was still locked!”

CHAPTER SEVEN

Cam told Mr. Day and Eric to go outside the office.

"Look through the window," Cam said. "What do you see?"

Eric said, "I see Mr. Day's office."

"I'm not even going to look," Mr. Day said. "I know what's in there."

Cam asked, "Do you see the cabinet?"

"Yes," Eric answered.

"Look through the cabinet doors," Cam told Eric. "What color are the walls?"

"Yellow," Eric said. "I can see the walls through the glass doors on the cabinet."

“Yes,” Cam said. “That’s what I saw when I looked in. I saw the walls because there’s no back to the cabinet. It’s open.”

“So what?” Mr. Day asked. “It’s always been open. No one can get into the cabinet from the back because it’s always against the wall.”

“Not always,” Cam said. “It wasn’t against the wall when the office was painted.”

"That's when the trophy was taken," Eric said. "The cabinet was away from the wall."

"And the painters left the door open," Mr. Day added. "They wanted fresh air in the office, to help the paint dry and to get rid of the smell."

A first grade teacher followed by his class came into the gym. The children were talking and laughing. Mr. Day turned and looked at them. The talking and laughing stopped.

Mr. Day told Cam and Eric, "I have to teach now. And you should get back to your class."

Cam and Eric left the gym.

"We solved part of the mystery," Eric said. "We know how the trophy was taken."

"But we don't know who took it," Cam said.

Cam and Eric walked into their classroom.

The children had their math textbooks and notebooks open. They were working quietly. Ms. Benson asked Cam and Eric to come to her desk.

"What happened?" she whispered. "Did you find the trophy?"

Cam and Eric told Ms. Benson everything. Then they sat in their seats. There was a math assignment on the board, problems one to twenty beginning on page fifty-four. Cam opened her book.

Cam read the first problem.

"Joan and Jane are traveling to the city."

Why? Cam wondered.

"The city is 150 miles away."

Why did someone steal the tennis trophy? Cam asked herself.

"Joan is traveling by bus. Jane is traveling by train."

Because it's made of silver, and silver is valuable, Cam thought. *That's why the trophy was stolen.*

"The bus travels at a steady 30 miles an hour. It makes no stops. The train travels at 60 miles an hour. It makes six 20 minute

stops. Who gets to the city first, Joan or Jane?"

Jane gets to the city first, Cam wrote. *Jane gets to the city in four and a half hours. Joan gets there in five hours.*

Cam read the next problem.

"Two stores have a sale on silver vases. In one store, the vases are $150 each. In the other store, vases are $200 each, but if you buy two, you get the third for free."

Three vases, Cam thought.

"Which store sells the vases for the lowest price?"

The lowest price, Cam thought. *That's easy. It's the buy-two-get-one-free store. But someone might not want three vases.*

Hey, Cam thought. *Three silver vases. Three silver trophies.*

That's it!

Cam closed her eyes and said, *"Click!"*

She looked at the picture she had in her head of Mr. Day's cabinet.

"That's it!" she said again. This time she said it aloud. "I think I know who took the tennis trophy."

CHAPTER EIGHT

"What's it?" Eric asked.

"The three vases," Cam answered. "That gave me the solution."

"That's an easy one," Eric said. "The vases are cheaper in the buy-two-get-one-free store. But who wants three vases? Who has that many flowers?"

"I'm not talking about vases," Cam told Eric. "I'm talking about Mr. Day's trophies."

Ms. Benson had walked to the back of the room. She stood by Cam's desk.

"Why aren't you working?" she asked Cam.

Ms. Benson turned and looked at Eric.

"Neither of you has done much work today."

"She solved the mystery," Eric said. "Cam knows who took the trophy."

"It's the three vases that gave me the answer," Cam said. "Mr. Day had three trophies. They were all made of silver. But someone reached in through the back of the cabinet and took just the tennis trophy."

"Maybe the thief was in a hurry," Ms. Benson said. "Maybe, just as he grabbed the tennis trophy, he heard someone coming and ran off."

Cam said, "Maybe *she* only wanted the tennis trophy."

"Why?" Ms. Benson asked.

"She?" Eric asked.

"Yes," Cam said. "Maybe *she* thought the tennis trophy was hers."

"You think Ms. Green took the trophy?" Eric asked.

"Yes," Cam said. "She thinks she deserved to win the tournament."

"She *did* deserve to win," Ms. Benson said. "Mr. Day's serve was out."

"Can we go to Ms. Green's room?" Cam asked. "Can we ask her if she took the trophy?"

"Not now," Ms. Benson said. "School is almost over. Do your work. After school we'll all go to Ms. Green and ask her."

"We'll miss our bus," Eric said.

"I'll drive you home. I'll call your parents and tell them. I'm sure they won't mind."

Ms. Benson went to the front of the room. Cam and Eric looked in their math books again. They worked quietly until the school bell rang.

"It's about time!" Danny called out. "I've learned enough."

Danny and the other children put their books away. They went to the closet and put on their jackets. Cam and Eric did, too. They all followed Ms. Benson outside.

"We're not going home on the bus," Cam and Eric told Mrs. Lane, their bus driver.

Cam, Eric, and Ms. Benson waited for the buses to drive off. Then they went to the music room to see Ms. Green.

They didn't have to ask her if she took the tennis trophy. It was on her desk.

"That's Mr. Day's trophy," Eric said.

"I just borrowed it," Ms. Green said. "I left a note."

The trophy had a large base. Set on top

Beethoven

was a small silver figure of a tennis player.

"Mr. Day didn't see your note," Cam said. "We spent all day looking for the trophy."

"I did leave a note," Ms. Green said. She took the trophy from the desk. "I'll show it to you," she said as she walked into the hall.

Cam, Eric, and Ms. Benson followed Ms. Green to the gym. Mr. Day was in his office.

"There it is!" Mr. Day said. "There's my trophy. *You* took it!"

Ms. Green gave it to Mr. Day.

"But I left you a note," she said.

"I have lots of notes here," Mr. Day said. He searched through the many papers, newspapers, and magazines on his desk and on the floor.

Then he pulled out a lined sheet of paper.

"That's it," Ms Green said.

Mr. Day read the note aloud.

"'I borrowed the tennis trophy. I want to see how it looks in my room. Don't worry. I'll bring it back. Doris Green.'

"Then you added a postscript. 'I still think the ball was out. We should play another match and see who really is the better player.'"

Mr. Day looked up from the note.

"Sure," he said. "Let's have another match."

"Fine," Ms. Green said. "But this time, I don't want Dr. Prell to be the umpire."

Ms. Benson said, "Cam should be the umpire. If the ball bounces near the line, she'll just go, *'Click.'* She'll take a mental picture of the ball. She can look at the picture she has in her head and know if it's in or out."

Mr. Day and Ms. Green set the game for the next day after school with Cam Jansen as the umpire.

Mr. Day set the trophy on his desk.

"Whoever wins the match," he said, "wins the trophy."

CHAPTER NINE

The next afternoon, a large crowd of teachers, parents, and children sat on the benches beside the school tennis court. Dr. Prell, the principal, was there. Cam's and Eric's parents were there, too. Cam sat by the net on a high umpire's chair. Eric stood along the side, ready to get balls that were out of play.

Cam tossed a coin to see who would serve first. Ms. Green won the toss.

Cam watched the game closely. Each time the ball bounced close to the line, Cam called it "In" or "Out." She also said, *"Click!"*

When Mr. Day or Ms. Green complained that she made the wrong call, Cam said, *"Click!"* again. She looked at the picture she had in her head.

There were no arguments. Mr. Day and Ms. Green agreed that Cam was a great umpire.

"I won't argue with a camera," Ms. Green said, "even a mental camera."

It was a close match. Both Mr. Day and Ms. Green were good players. When the match ended, they smiled and shook hands. They looked forward to the next time they would play tennis—and the next teachers' tournament.

A Cam Jansen Memory Game

Take another look at the picture opposite page 1. Study it. Blink your eyes and say, "*Click!*" Then turn back to this page and answer these questions. Please, first study the picture, *then* look at the questions.

1. What is written on the banner above Mr. Day's head?
2. Are there any pockets in Eric's shirt?
3. Is Cam's hair in a ponytail?
4. How many people are in the picture, 8, 10, or 12?
5. Is there a basketball net in the picture?
6. Who is wearing a checked shirt?
7. How many children are wearing hats?